I0816454

UFO SIGHTINGS EXPOSED!

by Megan Cooley Peterson

Published by Spark, an imprint of Capstone
1710 Roe Crest Drive, North Mankato, Minnesota 56003
capstonepub.com

Library of Congress Cataloging-in-Publication Data is available on the Library of Congress website

ISBN: 9781666357158 (hardcover)
ISBN: 9781666357165 (ebook PDF)

Summary: Readers will be riveted by curious tales of UFO sightings while also learning the facts about each claim.

Editorial Credits
Editor: Mandy Robbins; Designer: Heidi Thompson; Media Researchers: Jo Miller and Pam Mitsakos; Production Specialist: Tori Abraham

Image Credits
Alamy: Chronicle, 14, Pictorial Press Ltd, 16, World History Archive, 9; Getty Images: cosmin4000, 19, James Marshall, 24, Manuel Manca, 21, Maxiphoto, 23, PATRICK T. FALLON, 11; Shutterstock: Anzhela Perepichka, 28, CECIL BO DZWOWA, 20, Cheri Alguire, 10, Chris Harvey, 25, Fer Gregory, 17, Marko Aliaksandr, Cover, 2, 5, MWaits, 7, Studio-M, 29, wlkellar, 13, Zita Stankova, 15; U.S. Army photo by Staff Sgt. Pablo N. Piedra, 27

Printed and bound in the USA. PO 5986

TABLE OF CONTENTS

Words in **bold** are in the glossary.

MYSTERIES IN THE SKY

Something strange zips through the sky. Is it a plane? A **drone**? A shooting star? People report **UFOs** all the time. Some people think space aliens fly them. But is there any proof? Check out the facts and decide for yourself.

CRASH AT ROSWELL

It was June 1947. Mac Brazel and his son were driving near their home outside of Roswell, New Mexico. It looked like an object had crashed on their farmland. Bits of rubber, silver fabric, and sticks lay on the ground. Mac had never seen anything like it before.

UFO CRASH SITE
UFO Museum - 114 N. Main - Roswell

Mac called the police. The Roswell sheriff and a military **officer** came to the farm. They looked at the objects. The officer said they were part of a flying disc. Had aliens landed?

FACT

The *Roswell Daily Record* newspaper reported that the object was a flying saucer.

an officer inspecting the UFO wreckage

The U.S. War Department said it was not a spacecraft. It was pieces from a downed **weather balloon**. Not everyone believed that story.

Today, many people say an alien craft really did crash near Roswell. They visit the city to search for proof.

MYSTERY AT FALCON LAKE

May 20, 1967, started out as a normal day for Stefan Michalak. He was digging for **quartz** near Falcon Lake. It is in Manitoba, Canada. Around noon, some geese started honking. Stefan looked toward the sound. A metal object had just landed nearby. It was shaped like a disc.

Falcon Lake, Manitoba, Canada

A door opened on the object. Stefan saw bright lights inside. He moved closer, but the door shut. Hot gas burst out of the object. It hit Stefan and burned through his shirt. He fell to the ground. Then the object flew away.

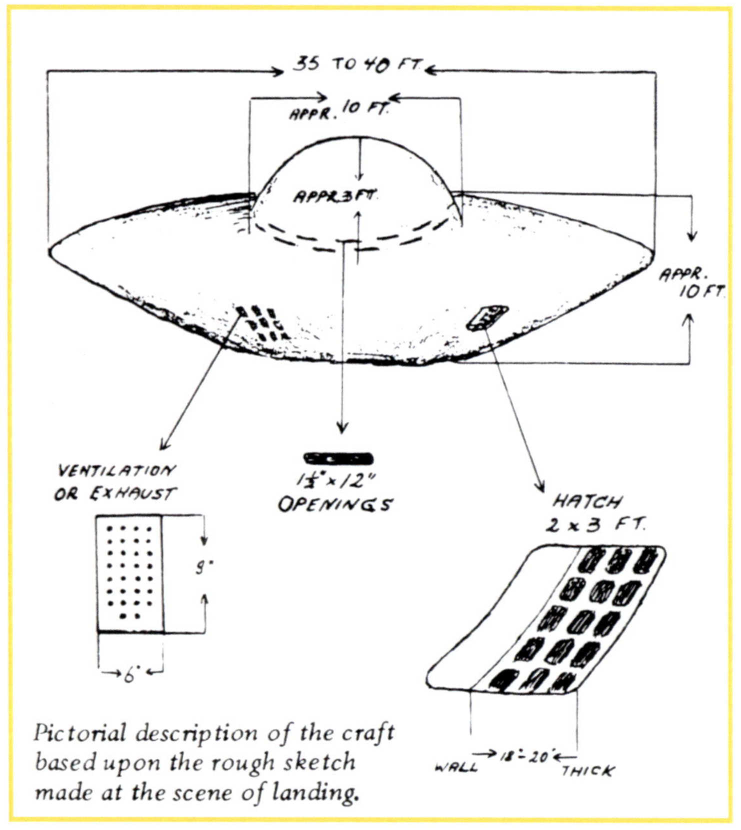

Pictorial description of the craft based upon the rough sketch made at the scene of landing.

FACT

Stefan thought the object might have been a secret U.S. military aircraft.

Stefan felt sick for months. He couldn't eat. He lost weight. He had burn marks on his chest. They would go away and come back.

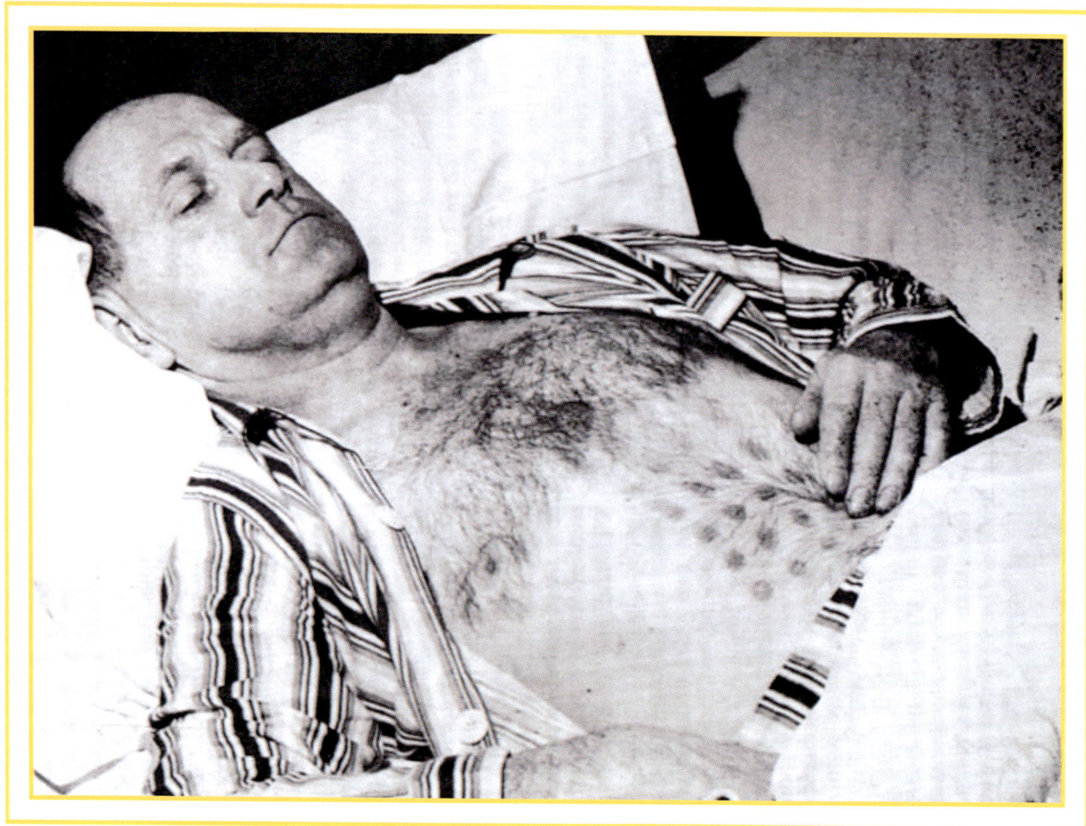

Doctors couldn't find anything wrong with Stefan. What had he seen that day in the woods?

STRANGE SCHOOL DAY

In September 1994, children at a school in Zimbabwe got a shock. An object flew overhead while they played outside. The silver disc landed near some trees. A creature dressed in black got out. It looked at the children with large black eyes. Then it got back into the object and flew away.

About 60 children said they saw the UFO. But teachers and staff saw nothing. They had been in a meeting.

Had the kids imagined what they saw? Other adults in the area did report a bright light in the sky.

A SPEEDY UFO

In 2004, two U.S. Navy pilots were flying off the coast of California. Some strange aircraft had been seen in the area. Using **radar**, the pilots spotted one of them. The white, oval-shaped craft was 40 feet long. It had no wings or **rotors**. The pilots couldn't understand how it flew without them.

0
10
20
25
N42.2104 W22.5251

The craft **hovered** just above the water. The water below it bubbled. One pilot flew toward it. But the object zoomed away. The pilot had never seen anything fly that fast. Was it an alien spaceship or something else? No one knows.

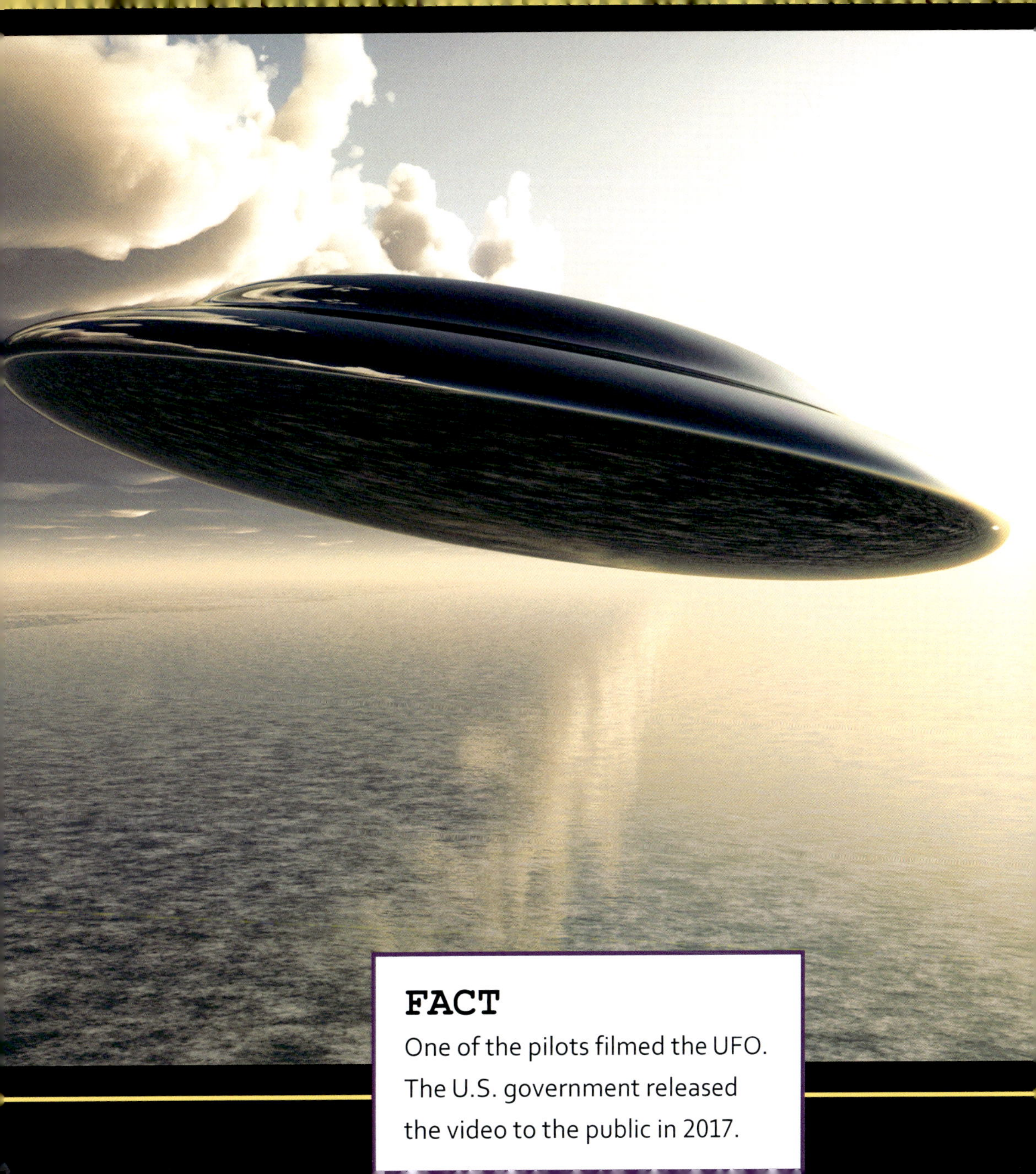

FACT

One of the pilots filmed the UFO. The U.S. government released the video to the public in 2017.

ENCOUNTER AT THE AIRPORT

In April 2013, something odd happened in Aguadilla, Puerto Rico. An airplane was about to take off from the airport. Suddenly, an object flew over the runway. It was about 5 feet long. It had a reddish-pink light. The object flew up to 120 miles per hour.

The object then moved over the ocean. It dipped in and out of the water as it flew. Then it split into two parts. Both parts kept flying. Then they disappeared.

Scientists studied video of this UFO.
They said it wasn't a drone or plane.
Was it an alien spacecraft?

Glossary

drone (DROHN)—an unmanned, remote-controlled aircraft

hover (HUHV-er)—to remain in one place in the air

officer (OF-uh-sur)—someone who is in charge of other people

quartz (KWARTZ)—a very common, hard, glossy mineral

radar (RAY-dar)—a device that uses radio waves to track the location of objects

rotor (ROH-tur)—a set of rotating blades that lift an aircraft off the ground

UFO—an object in the sky thought to be a spaceship from another planet; UFO stands for unidentified flying object

weather balloon (WHE-thur BUH-loon)—a balloon that carries instruments into the sky to gather weather data in the air

Read More

Baker, Theo. *Aliens and UFOs*. Vero Beach, FL: Rourke Educational Media, 2019.

Chanez, Katie. *UFO Sightings*. North Mankato, MN: Capstone, 2020.

Hoena, Blake. *The Roswell UFO Incident*. Minneapolis: Bellwether Media, Inc., 2020.

Internet Sites

Do You Believe in UFOs?
wonderopolis.org/wonder/do-you-believe-in-ufos

UFO No Longer Unidentified
nasa.gov/vision/space/travelinginspace/no_ufo.html

What Exactly Are UFOs?
cbc.ca/kidscbc2/the-feed/what-exactly-are-ufos

Index

About the Author

Megan Cooley Peterson has been an avid reader and writer since she was a little girl. She has written nonfiction children's books about topics ranging from urban legends to gross animal facts. She lives in Minnesota with her husband, daughter, and cuddly kitty.